# Star Sisters
## and the
# Great Skate

D1416904

Written by Jennifer Blecher

Illustrated by Anne Zimanski

Disclaimer: This is a work of fiction. Some characters within it are based on living persons. However, all actions, statements, and thoughts attributed to such characters, and all other events and incidents depicted in this work, are either the products of the author's imagination or are used in a fictitious manner.

TO ELLA – FOR ALL THE INSPIRATION.

# Prologue

One thousand years ago, a mighty river
flowed through the ancient land of Illustria.
Past fields of wildflowers and through lush
green valleys, the river charted its winding

course.  Like all good rivers, it quenched

people's thirst and sustained the earth.  But

the river of Illustria did not flow with water

alone, it also flowed with magic.  This river

had the power to heal.

The royal family of Illustria was kind and

they invited the sick, the weak, and the

needy to drink from the river's shores.

From far and wide people came and, drop by drop, they were healed.

Until one day an evil Queen invaded Illustria, hoping to claim the river's powers for her own. Though she was able to defeat the royal family of Illustria and banish them from the land, she was not able to control the river. Sensing that there was no kindness in the evil Queen's soul, the river receded, its flowing waters becoming a trickling stream. Everyone thought the river's magic was gone forever. But everyone was wrong.

For before the evil Queen invaded, the King of Illustria had given his daughters, the princess sisters, necklaces made from star-shaped emeralds that were unearthed from the shores of the river. These necklaces gave the princesses the power to vanish and magically travel to far away lands where they would help spread kindness. The kingdom of Illustria is no more, but the necklaces have survived. And their magic lives on.

It lives around the necks of two regular girls named Coco and Lucy. New to their town and both a little lonely, Coco and Lucy met when they fell into the stream that was once Illustria's mighty river. Each girl was wearing one of the princesses' necklaces, only the emerald stars had turned to stone

stars.  A tiny fairy named Grissella, a lone

survivor from the days of Illustria, popped

out of a tree trunk to help Coco and Lucy understand that they had been brought together not by chance, but by fate. By magic. Of all the girls in the world, they had been chosen to carry on the mission of the royal family of Illustria: to spread kindness.

Though Coco and Lucy had their doubts, when they said a special chant the stone stars on their necklaces turned to glowing emerald stars and they were whisked away on a magical adventures, spreading kindness as they went. They don't know when the magic will come again, or where they'll be taken, but they know it will happen. For they are the Star Sisters. And they are ready!

# Chapter One

It was a cold and snowy winter day. Sleds zoomed down hills, snowflakes gathered on tree branches, and snowmen stood watch over the neighborhood. Next to one particularly fabulous snowman wearing a hot

pink scarf, lay Coco and Lucy. They were
on their backs making snow angels and
staring up into the cloudy sky.

"Twiddle dee, twiddle dum, I spy a sparkling drum," said Coco.

"Twiddle dee, twiddle dum, I see a candy cane, yum," said Lucy.

"Twiddle dee, twiddle dum, I feel a snow lump on my bum," said Coco.

Lucy giggled and sat up, the snow crunching and cracking under her shifting weight. "Good one," she said. "But now what? I'm bored."

How could Lucy be bored in such a winter wonderland? Well, there's one more thing you need to know about this particular snowy day. It wasn't the first snowy day, or the second, or the third, but the fourth snowy day in a row! And sometimes by the fourth snowy day in a row, even two girls who love to play outside can get a little bored.

"I don't know," said Coco. "Should we go to the forest to see Grissella? We could take a sled."

"No," said Lucy. "Grissella's probably still huddled up inside her tree trunk. Plus, she'll just tell us to be patient. And if I have to be patient for another second, my head is going to fly right off and hit the sky."

"Twiddle dee, twiddle dum, I'll reattach your head with bubble gum," said Coco.

"Thanks," said Lucy, laughing. "But I still hate waiting."

Coco nodded and began drawing stars in the snow with her glove. It had been a while

since their last adventure as Star Sisters and it was hard not knowing when the magic would transport them once again. Plus, every little thing reminded them of what they were waiting for!

The green peas on Lucy's dinner plate were the exact color of the stars on their necklaces when they turned to emeralds. Every time Coco took a sip from the 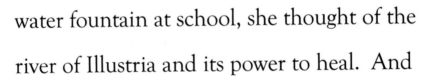 water fountain at school, she thought of the river of Illustria and its power to heal. And most important of all, when each girl woke up in the morning she still remembered that old feeling, the one of being a little lonely. Of wondering what the day would bring with no friend to play with. But then the haze of sleep would lift and the sun would peak through the crack in the curtains as if trying to sneak its way into the room and each girl would smile. For each would remember the other and know that the day would be a great one because her best friend would be in it.

"I have an idea," said Coco, jumping up from the snow. "Let's go ice skating. I'm sure my mom will take us."

"I've never been ice skating," said Lucy.

"Me neither," said Coco.

"But we are pretty good at new things," said Lucy.

Coco laughed. "Especially magical new things! Come on, let's go find my mom."

Two sets of snow pants, long underwear, helmets, gloves, socks, warm jackets, and laced up ice skates later, the girls were skating. It sure was slippery out there on the ice, but before long their legs stopped behaving like wiggly strands of spaghetti and they were gliding along together.

Left foot, right foot, left foot, right foot. Coco and Lucy were having so much fun they didn't notice that somehow they were the only skaters left on the ice.

It wasn't until the lights dimmed and the music stopped that they realized something strange was happening.

"Do you think this is what we've been waiting for?" asked Coco. "Do you think the magic is coming?"

"Maybe," said Lucy. "Let's give it a try."

Coco and Lucy held hands. The minute their fingers touched they knew that yes, this was it, the moment they'd been waiting for. How could they tell? Well, it was kind of like the feeling you get on the morning of your birthday. When you just know deep inside your belly that it's not another regular day. So Coco and Lucy said their special

chant:

"We're star sisters, friends forever.

Through thick and thin, we're both in."

And sure enough, the stars on their

necklaces started to glow. Like chocolate

sauce spreading over a fresh scoop of vanilla

ice cream, the stone stars changed into

brilliant green emerald stars. The light from

the emeralds combined and started to circle

around the two girls, like a halo of bright

sparkles. One rumble later, Coco and Lucy

were still in their skates standing in the

middle of an ice skating rink. But it was not

the same ice skating rink. Not even close.

# Chapter Two

"Oh good, you're here," said a woman as she skated over to Coco and Lucy. She was carrying a clipboard and wearing a large puffy jacket. "I was beginning to get worried. I'm Ms. Jane. Are you ready?"

"Um, ready for what exactly?" asked Coco in a normal voice that actually sounded quite loud. For the girls were standing in the middle of an enormous ice arena (which is a fancy word for stadium, which is a fancy word for a really, really, really big ice skating rink). Even the tiniest noise carried across the smooth surface of the ice and echoed off the hundreds of empty plastic seats that circled all around.

"Your instructions, of course," said Ms. Jane. "The skating competition starts tomorrow. The skaters have been here all week practicing and tickets sold out months ago. We're expecting a huge crowd."

"Competition?" asked Lucy.

"Crowd?" asked Coco.

"Girls, why do you look so confused?" said Ms. Jane. "This is the United States National Figure Skating Championships. The best ice skaters in America are competing for a spot in the Olympics. You two have been chosen from all the young skaters in the entire country to be our sweepers."

"Oh, right," said Lucy. "Sweepers, of course. We knew that." She looked at Coco and shrugged her shoulders. *What in the world was a sweeper?*

Ms. Jane continued, "Those emerald necklaces will look great on the ice. Good choice. Are you ready to begin?"

Coco and Lucy squeezed each other's hand and nodded. Sure, it was a little scary to be magically transported to somewhere unknown, especially somewhere big and cold and unknown. But when you had a friend by your side and a magical star glowing on your neck, it was easy to replace any scary thoughts with really exciting ones. Especially when Ms. Jane told them more about what a sweeper does.

"Being a sweeper is a very important job," explained Ms. Jane. "After every skater finishes her routine, or program, as we call it in ice skating, fans like to throw flowers and gifts, like stuffed animals or cards, onto the ice. It's the sweeper's job to skate onto the ice, collect all the items, and bring them to the skater who will be waiting for her score from the judges."

"Now, being a sweeper is not easy," Jane continued. "Not easy at all. You have to make sure to get every little thing off the ice. A single petal from a rose or loose thread from a stuffed animal could cause the next skater to trip and fall. Remember, these skaters are moving incredibly fast on really thin blades. The tiniest scrap left on the ice could be disastrous. So be very, very careful that you get every last bit."

"Don't worry, Ms. Jane," said Coco. "We'll get every last itty bitty bit."

"Yep," said Lucy. "We'll be the best itty bitty bit getters that you've ever seen."

"Good," said Ms. Jane with a nod. "Now, why don't you take off your skates and stay and watch the top skaters practice. Keep an eye on Nina Kerrington and Tara Harling. They're the favorites to win the competition. I bet one of them is going to be the next Olympic gold medalist, the highest honor in the entire sport of figure skating. Just you wait and see."

# Chapter Three

Coco and Lucy skated to the barriers, took off their ice skates, and climbed up into the tippy top level of the stands. *Chug a lug, chug a lug, huffff*, went the Zamboni machine as it cleaned the ice, leaving in its wake ice so shiny and smooth that it looked like glass.

Moments later, six skaters took the ice. Or should we say stormed the ice? Or maybe attacked the ice? For while each skater moved with the grace of a ballerina, her arms spread wide and fingertips stretched to their longest points, there was a power in her strokes and a focus in her eyes that made Coco and Lucy sit up just a tad bit straighter.

These skaters may have been wearing delicate outfits made of lace and chiffon, but their muscles were strong, their bodies confident, and pretty soon they were flying

through the air. Axels, lutzes, flips, loops, toe loops, and salchows. They launched themselves up, up, up, twisting round and round in tight circles, only to land on one foot in a graceful backward glide.

"Pretty awesome, right?" said a girl's voice coming from behind where Coco and Lucy were sitting.

Coco and Lucy nodded. "Amazing," said Coco.

"I'm Sara," said the girl. "See the skater wearing all black? The one with the blond hair and bangs? That's my big sister, Tara. Isn't she the greatest? I just love her so much."

Coco and Lucy watched as Tara bent her left knee deeply and lifted off facing forward, spinning around three and a half times in the air before landing backwards. Tara pumped her first into the air in excitement.

"That's called a triple axel," explained Sara. "Tara's the only skater in the

competition who can land that jump.
That's why she's going to win tomorrow."

"Which skater is Nina?" asked Lucy.

"Oh, she's the one with a brown pony
tail, wearing the white dress," said Sara.
"She's really good, too.  I guess."  Sara
sighed.

"She's not just good," said Coco.  "She's
incredible."

"Fantastic," said Lucy.

"Incredible, fantastic, and amazing all
mixed together in a yummy milkshake with
whipped cream and sprinkles and gummy
bears on top," said Coco.

"Don't forget the cherry," said Lucy, smiling.

"Silly me," said Coco.

Nina was doing fast backward crossovers across the ice. Then she stepped forward onto her left leg, raising her right leg high with her hand at her knee.

"That's her signature spiral," said Sara. "She does it in every program."

"No wonder Ms. Jane thinks Tara and Nina are the best skaters in the competition," said Lucy.

"That's what everyone thinks," said Sara. "But I know Tara's going to win. I just know it."

"How do you know it?" asked Coco.

"Because it's been her dream to compete in the Olympics since we were little girls," said Sara. "She trains every day and practices her spins and jumps for hours at a time. Even if her belly hurts or she keeps falling, Tara just tries harder and harder until she gets it right. So I just know she'll win."

"It looks like all these skaters practice a lot," said Lucy as she watched Nina spin in a fast circle with her back arched, her arms raised high.

"Probably," said Sara with a shrug. Her eyes looked down at the floor and her shoulders hunched over. "I just really hope it's Tara who wins."

"Don't worry, Sara," said Lucy. "I'm sure you'll be cheering the loudest of anyone in the whole stadium tomorrow. That will definitely help Tara skate her best."

"I just wish there was something more I could do," said Sara. "Tara helps me all the time. She lifts me up to get my favorite sparkly shirt when it's in the top drawer, she pours me a glass of milk when I'm thirsty, and when my favorite teddy bear got a hole in his paw, she sewed him right up. She didn't even need help threading the needle. But I never know what to do to help her. Oh well. I'm sure I'll think of something. Gotta go. Bye, bye."

Sara hippity-hopped down the steep steps of the stadium. Coco and Lucy waved good-bye and continued watching the other skaters practice.

# Chapter Four

The next day the ice skating rink was the opposite of cold and empty. Instead of the lonely sound of a single voice echoing in the stands, noise seemed to rise from every nook and cranny.

Photographers with huge black cameras sat along the edge of the ice.  *Click, click, click* went their cameras with lightning fast speed. Spectators filled every seat, their clothes creating a wild blur of color and their voices combining to form a muffled roar.  And servers carrying huge trays of popcorn and cotton

candy

walked up

and down

the aisles,

leaving the

delicious smell of butter and sugar in their wake.

Below all this excitement, underneath the seats and down a long hallway that blocked out much of the noise, Coco and Lucy were in the locker room watching the skaters get ready to compete.

Earlier in the day Ms. Jane had dropped off new skating dresses for Coco and Lucy to wear when they picked up the flowers and gifts off the ice. The dresses were white with green chiffon skirts and green puffed sleeves.

"I thought the green accents would really bring out the emeralds on your necklaces," said Ms. Jane. And holy moly spicy guacamole, Jane was right. Their necklaces were glowing brighter than ever before.

Coco and Lucy watched closely as the skaters stretched their arms and legs, as they bent their necks left, then right, then left again. Some skaters put their hands over their eyes and others did deep knee bends. It seemed as if every skater was in her own little world, warming up her body for the big event.

"Look," said Lucy. "There's Nina. She looks like she's ready to skate her heart out."

It was true. Nina's thick brown hair was pulled back in a tight bun. She wore a sparkly, long-sleeved gold dress that glimmered with every movement. Even though she was about to skate in one of the biggest competitions of her life, she took the time to smile at Coco and Lucy.

"Are you two girls the sweepers?" asked Nina.

Coco and Lucy nodded.

"That's so exciting," said Nina. "You look like you'll be great sweepers."

"Thanks," said Coco. "I hope so."

"I know so," said Nina. "And if you get a little nervous out there just wiggle your toes. That's what I do. It reminds me that it's just me and my ice skates that matter. Not the judges, or the other skaters, or anything else. Just me and my skates."

Nina gave them a thumbs-up and walked away to lace her skates. Coco and Lucy looked around while they wiggled their toes for practice. Tara was listening to music on her headphones and punching her arms in the air, like a boxer taking jabs at an imaginary opponent.  Coaches were whispering last minute advice to their skaters, and officials with plastic badges hanging from their necks were checking their watches.

Let's just say it was a little coo-coo-crazy back there.  Actually, it was *very* coo-coo-crazy.  Which helps to explain why it felt like all of a sudden it was "go" time.

# Chapter Five

"Remember girls, keep an eye out for leaves from flowers, buttons from stuffed animals, scraps of paper from cards, anything," said Ms. Jane as she led Coco and Lucy towards the ice. "It doesn't matter how tiny. Any little thing on the ice could cause a skater to fall and ruin everything that she's been training for."

"Got it," said Coco. "Look for the itty bitty."

"Yep," said Lucy. "Nothing's going to get past us. Not even the ittiest bittiest bit."

"Good," said Ms. Jane. "I know you can do it. Now, enjoy the competition." Ms. Jane drew back a curtain, allowing Coco and Lucy to see the full arena for the first time.

"Wow," said Coco.

"I've never seen so many people," said Lucy.

"I think I'm nervous," said Coco.

"Me, too," said Lucy.

Now, feeling nervous is not an easy feeling. But feeling nervous while standing on ice skates is a tad bit harder. The girls' legs shook as they tried to balance on the thin steel blades, their hearts raced, and their eyes darted all around.

Coco and Lucy tried to focus on wiggling their toes, but the wiggling made them even wobblier. But then they grabbed hands. (Partly for balance, true, but also for comfort). And when their hands connected they knew in their hearts that they would be fine. Because although they were two very small girls standing on two very thin pairs of blades, they were strong. And tough. And they had each other.

A voice announced that Tara Harling would be the first skater to compete. Tara smiled and waved as the whole crowd cheered her name. *Ta-ra, Ta-ra, Ta-ra.* But there was one voice that rose above the others. "I love you, Tara," yelled Sara. "You can do it."

Tara took a deep breath as she found her starting point on the ice. Then her music began and Tara started to fly. With great power she spun and jumped and moved in all directions. She landed her triple lutz, triple flip, and triple loop, but then came the moment that everyone was waiting for. Her triple axel. The hardest jump that any skater was attempting in the entire competition and most people believed that if Tara could land her triple axel, she would win the gold medal.

"Here she goes," whispered Lucy as Tara stepped forward on her left leg and started the jump. Once, twice, three times she spun in the air. She had almost completed the final half of the very last rotation when something in her body twitched, maybe an arm or a leg, and she fell hard to the ice.

It was terrible. Poor Tara. But she got up, brushed herself off, and kept skating. She finished her program with a smile on her face. Tara didn't land the triple axel, but she still skated well and the crowd showed their appreciation by showering the ice with gifts.

"Now it's our turn to shine," said Lucy as she and Coco stepped onto the ice. They moved around as gracefully as they could, picking up all the flowers and stuffed animals and bringing them over to Tara who was waiting for her scores. Then, just to be sure, Coco and Lucy took one final sweep of the ice, looking for all the itty bitties that

Ms. Jane was so worried about.

"All clear," said Coco as she came back to the edge of the ice.

"Definitely," agreed Lucy. Tara's scores from the judges were good, but not great. She looked a little disappointed. But she took a deep breath and waved to the crowd with a big smile as she walked back to the locker room to take off her skates.

# Chapter Six

The next skater to take the ice was Nina. Coco and Lucy watched as she whispered some last words to her coach. Then her name was announced and, with a big smile and her head held high, she skated onto the ice to warm up her legs.

"Oh, I just love Nina," said Lucy.

"Me, too," said Coco. "She's so graceful. And she doesn't even look nervous. Not even with all these millions and billions and gazillions of people watching her."

Lucy laughed. "You forgot trillions," she said.

"Silly me," said Coco. "Millions and billions and trillions and gazillions of people."

"Much better," said Lucy.

The entire arena grew silent as Nina skated to her starting point. The tiniest noise can distract an ice skater and even though there were millions and billions and trillions and gazillions of people watching, they all knew that this was an important moment.

Nina's eyes were focused and she was breathing deeply. She looked ready to give it her best shot. But just then, Lucy noticed something. Something reaching out over the barrier. Or maybe not something, but someone. Someone's arm to be exact. Just as quickly as it appeared, it disappeared.

"Did you see that?" Lucy asked Coco.

"See what?" said Coco.

"Someone leaned over the ice," said Lucy. "I swear."

"I didn't see it, but I believe you," said Coco. "Who do you think it was?"

"I don't know," said Lucy. "It looked like a person leaning over the edge of the barrier. But it happened so fast that I'm not sure."

Coco was about to suggest that they tell Ms. Jane, when an awful thing happened. Nina fell. *Thump.* Her body hit the ice and she curled up into a ball clutching her right knee.

"Oh no!" cried Lucy. "Come on! We're the only ones nearby with ice skates on. Nina needs our help."

Coco and Lucy skated over to Nina and tried to help her stand up, but she was in too much pain. "It's no use, girls," said Nina. "My knee. My knee really hurts."

"Oh, Nina," said Lucy. "We're so sorry."

"It's not your fault," winced Nina. "I just tripped. It happens sometimes."

And that's when Coco saw it, lying there on the ice – a single pink rose petal right at the spot where Nina fell.

"Oh no," cried Coco. "It *was* our fault. Nina, you tripped on a rose petal that was left on the ice.  It was our job to make sure the ice was clean."

Nina looked down at the rose petal. "How could something so little ruin all my dreams?" she said and burst into tears.

"Something so itty bitty," said Lucy, faintly.

# Chapter Seven

After a few minutes, Nina was able to
make her way off the ice. The competition
was delayed while a doctor examined her
hurt knee. Meanwhile, Coco and Lucy felt
awful.

"It's all our fault," said Coco. "I thought we were sent here to help. And look what happened, we ruined everything."

"So much for our magical necklaces," said Lucy. "This never would have happened to the princess sisters of Illustria. They spread kindness throughout the land, not pain."

Coco and Lucy were so upset that they almost didn't hear the sound of crying coming from behind them. But when they turned around they saw Sara sitting next to a pile of pink roses, tears running down her cheeks. "It wasn't your fault," said Sara. "It was my fault. All mine."

"Sara," said Coco. "What are you talking about?"

"I did something terrible," said Sara. "Something really, really bad."

Coco and Lucy paused and thought back to some mistakes they'd recently made. Because after all, everyone makes mistakes. Even Star Sisters.

"Worse than hiding Halloween candy in your closet?" asked Lucy.

"Worse," said Sara.

"Even if you forget about the candy and the chocolate melts all over your clean underwear?" asked Lucy.

"I'm afraid so," said Sara.

"Worse than painting your dog's nails hot pink?" asked Coco.

"Way worse," said Sara.

Coco and Lucy looked at each other with eyes wide open. "Sara," said Lucy. "What did you do?"

Sara took a deep breath. "When Tara fell on her triple axel I got worried that she wouldn't make it to the Olympics," she said. "So I decided to throw a rose petal onto the ice. I thought that if Nina fell too then Tara would have a better chance of winning. Skaters fall all the time. I didn't think she'd get so hurt. I didn't think I would feel so badly."

"So that was your arm that I saw reaching over the ice?" asked Lucy. "You did this on purpose."

Sara nodded her head and wiped her eyes. "I was going to give the roses to Tara. That's why I had them. But then this idea just came to me. I don't know what I was thinking. I wasn't thinking. It was a terrible mistake."

"Oh, Sara, said Coco. "This is really, really bad. We have to tell someone."

"I know," said Sara. "Just please let me tell Tara first. I don't want her to hear it from anyone else."

# Chapter Eight

Sara, Coco, and Lucy found Tara in the locker room wiping off her ice skates.

"Did you guys hear what just happened?" asked Tara. "Nina fell. She hurt her knee and might not be able to compete. It's really bad."

"I more than heard," said Sara. "I'm the one responsible."

"What do you mean?" asked Tara.

"I made her fall," said Sara. "I threw a rose petal on the ice hoping that Nina would skate over it and trip. I didn't think she'd get hurt. I just really wanted you to win, Tara. I thought I was helping."

"Oh, Sara," said Tara, shaking her head. "It's not winning if you cheat. There's no glory in that."

"I know that now," said Sara. "I made a huge mistake. What do we do now?"

Coco and Lucy looked at each other and nodded. Suddenly, their entire reason for being at the ice skating competition became clear. They touched the emerald stars hanging around their necks and knew this was their chance to spread some kindness. "Now we need to find Nina and fix this," said Coco.

So off they went. They wandered down the long twisty-turny hallways of the arena until they found Nina sitting with the doctor and her coach. Nina's right knee was already tightly bandaged.

Sara was nervous. Not the good kind of nervous Coco and Lucy felt earlier, but the harder kind of nervous. The kind of nervous you feel when you've done something wrong and you're not quite sure how to make it right.

"Um, excuse me," said Sara in a quiet voice. "There's something I have to tell you."

"Who are you?" asked Nina.

"I'm Tara's sister," said Sara. "And I owe you an apology."

"This isn't a great time," said Nina.

"I know," said Sara. "That's why I'm here."

# Chapter Nine

Sara sat down and told Nina the whole

story. How she was so upset about Tara

falling on her triple axel and how she threw

the rose petal on the ice. How she didn't

mean for Nina to get so hurt. She said a lot of things, but do you want to know the most important thing she said? It was: "I made a big mistake. I'm sorry. I'm really, really sorry."

"I know you made a mistake," said Nina. "And I appreciate your apology. But that doesn't fix things. I'm still hurt, my chance at the Olympics, my dream, it's...it's gone."

"Maybe," said Coco. "But maybe not. Can Lucy and I talk to Nina alone?"

"I don't know if that's a good idea," said the doctor. "She's really hurt. She needs to stay perfectly still."

"Please," said Coco. "It will just take a minute."

"Okay," said the doctor. "But just one minute."

"What are you thinking?" whispered Lucy as everyone else walked away.

"I'm thinking that when all else fails, magic prevails," said Coco. "Remember how our emeralds came from the magical river in Illustria? The river that had the power to heal the sick? Well, maybe there's still enough healing power left to fix Nina's knee."

"But we never take our necklaces off," said Lucy. "What if they stop glowing and turn back to stone? What will we do then?"

"What will Nina do if we don't help her?" said Coco.

"Good point," said Lucy. "We're Star Sisters. We have to try."

"What are you two whispering about?" asked Nina.

"We think we know a way to help," said Coco. "But you're going to have to close your eyes and trust us, okay?"

Nina thought for a moment. "Okay," she said. "What do I have to lose?"

As Nina closed her eyes, Coco and Lucy took off their necklaces and held the stones over Nina's knee. Moments later, a green light spread over her knee and she smiled. "Hey," said Nina. "I think my knee feels a little better."

"Better enough to compete?" asked Coco.

"I think so," said Nina as she stood up and smiled. "I don't know what you two did, but I'm forever grateful. This skate is dedicated to you guys."

Nina walked to the ice. She stepped on slowly, with a bit of a tremble, but as she skated around something came over her, a kind of confidence that seemed to start at her heart and spread out to her chest, legs, and down her arms to the tips of her fingers. Nina gave the judges a thumbs up sign and told them she was ready to start. And would you believe it, she skated the best program of her life, nailing every jump and moving through her footwork section and spins with amazing precision. When she did her final spiral, the one she was known for with her leg raised high, her hand on her knee, her smile was so wide that it filled the entire arena.

# Chapter Ten

But poor Coco and Lucy, they sure had a

lot of things to clean off the ice.  The people

watching were so moved by Nina's

performance that they threw everything they

had down on the ice, including a baby's

pacifier. Silly baby! But the tricky thing

about ice skating (besides the actual jumping

through the air and landing on tiny blades)

is that deciding who wins is not up to the

fans, a clock, or a measuring stick.

It's up to the judges. The nine people who sit in the front row wearing large coats and serious expressions. As Nina sat next to her coach, waiting for the judges to score her performance, she hugged Coco and Lucy.

"I don't know what you girls did," said Nina. "But I know it was magic. You gave me the chance to compete and I'm so grateful."

Coco and Lucy were happy for Nina, but something still didn't feel quite right. Like there was a missing piece of a puzzle lost between the couch cushions or eaten by the family dog. "I feel like there's something else we need to do," said Coco.

"I agree," said Lucy. "It doesn't feel like our mission is over. But what else can we do? We fixed Nina's knee and she got to compete, to shoot for her dreams. Isn't that what we were brought here to do?"

"I don't think so," said Coco. "Remember, the princess sisters of Illustria spread kindness.

These necklaces found us because we're supposed to help carry out that  mission. We made Nina's knee feel better, but that was magic, not kindness. There has to be something more."

Just then, the judges announced their scores. Nina won the ice skating competition! Tara came in second. They both qualified to compete in the Olympic games.

Ms. Jane rushed up to Coco and Lucy. "Girls, you have one last job," she said in a hurried voice. "The skaters are going to receive their medals in the center of the ice. I need one of you to skate the medals out to them and place them around their necks."

"Just one of us?" asked Coco.

"Just one," confirmed Ms. Jane.

Coco turned to Lucy. "I think I have an idea," she said. "Let's find Sara."

Minutes later, it was Sara who skated the medals onto the ice. As Sara stood in front of Nina with the gold medal in her hands, Nina looked confused. "Not again," she said.

"Never again," said Sara. "I learned my lesson. Sports is not about who wins or loses, it's about everyone trying their best. Cheating just ruins everything."

"That's exactly right," said Nina.

"I was thinking that maybe I'd like to start learning to be an ice skater," said Sara. "And I was wondering if you would teach me how to do your signature spiral. That

way I would think about you and the lessons I learned every time I skate."

"You know what?" said Nina. "It would be an honor. I think if we both get to know each other, we could be good friends."

Coco and Lucy gave each other a high five. "Now that's kindness," said Lucy. "I

think it's finally time to go home."

"Yep," said Coco. "It's time."

They took one last look at the ice skating rink where so many dreams had hung in the air like clouds. One of those dreams almost didn't come true, but thanks to Coco and Lucy, it did. Both Nina and Tara were going to compete in the Olympics. And who knows, maybe one day Sara would as well.

Coco and Lucy found a quiet spot, held hands, and said their favorite words:

*"We're Star Sisters, friends forever.*
*Through thick and thin, we're both in."*

And a flash and a blink later they were back at their local ice skating rink on that cold snowy day. The emerald stars on their necklaces turned back to stones, but they didn't mind. Coco and Lucy knew the stars would be shining bright again in no time.

## THE END

Can't get enough of the Star Sisters? You're in luck. See what else Coco and Lucy are up to...

Trina Fast loves to be up on stage with the microphone turned up high and her guitar in her hands. But when Trina writes a song about her friend Lake for the summer camp talent show that hurts Lake's feelings, she learns an important lesson about the power of her own voice.

It's summertime and Coco and Lucy are ready to dive into the swimming pool and another great adventure about the meaning of friendship.

It's the night before the royal wedding and all is not well in Luckingham Palace. When Princess-to-be Caroline and her sister Poppy have a fight over Poppy's wedding attire, both sisters feel their friendship being tested. Will the event the world has been waiting for be ruined? Not with the Star Sisters on the job!

Join Coco and Lucy as they save the day with the help of a friendly seamstress, some creative thinking, and a big helping of sisterly love.

**www.star-sisters.com**

Visit **www.star-sisters.com** for star necklaces, coloring pages, and all the latest info on where Coco and Lucy are popping up next.

**Westgate Publishing**

CPSIA information can be obtained
at www.ICGtesting.com
Printed in the USA
LVOW12s1601180716

496766LV00003B/740/P